Kids love reading
Choose Your

"The books [...]
the future to see what happens."

Katie Parker, age 10

"The adventures are really cool. Each adventure can be an adventure for you, but you are reading a book!"

Rebecca Frank, age 8

"These books are the best, everyone should read them."

McKenzie Tucker, age 11

"I love all the riddles, they are so fun! I did not know there were so many ways to go."

Charlotte Young, age 9

"*Choose Your Own Adventures* are full of adventure and mystery. You never know what's going to happen."

Benjamin Byrne, age 10

CHECK OUT CHOOSE YOUR OWN NIGHTMARE:
EIGHTH GRADE WITCH • BLOOD ISLAND • SNAKE INVASION

YOU MIGHT ALSO ENJOY THESE BESTSELLERS . . .

CHOOSE YOUR OWN ADVENTURE®

CHOOSE YOUR OWN ADVENTURE®

THE FLIGHT OF THE UNICORN

BY DEBORAH LERME GOODMAN

ILLUSTRATED BY SUZANNE NUGENT
COVER ILLUSTRATED BY MARCO CANNELLA

CHOOSECO
WAITSFIELD, VERMONT

Book design: Stacey Boyd, Big Eyedea Visual Design

For information regarding permission, write to:

CHOOSECO
P.O. Box 46
Waitsfield, Vermont 05673
www.cyoa.com

Publisher's Cataloging-In-Publication Data
(Prepared by The Donohue Group, Inc.)
Names: Goodman, Deborah Lerme, 1956- author. | Nugent, Suzanne,
illustrator. | Canella, Marco, illustrator.
Title: The flight of the unicorn / by Deborah Lerme Goodman ; illustrated by Suzanne Nugent ; cover illustrated by Marco Canella.
Other Titles: Choose your own adventure.
Description: Waitsfield, Vermont : Chooseco, [2022] | Interest age
level: 009-012. | Summary: "The sequel to The Rescue of the Unicorn
takes you on a fantastic quest through medieval Scotland to find your
missing pegacorn mentor, Dame Scotia. You believe she was kidnapped to
use her magic to create a pegacorn army. Will you and your newly
trained pegacorn, Liss, locate Dame Scotia in time to prevent a
possible war?"-- Provided by publisher.
Identifiers: ISBN 9781954232044
Subjects: LCSH: Unicorns--Scotland--Juvenile fiction. | Magic--Juvenile
fiction. | Kidnapping--Scotland--Juvenile fiction. | CYAC: Unicorns--
Scotland--Fiction. | Magic--Fiction. | Kidnapping--Scotland--Fiction. |
LCGFT: Choose-your-own stories.
Classification: LCC PZ7.G61358 Fl 2022 | DDC [Fic]--dc23

Published simultaneously in the United States and Canada

Printed in in the United States

10 9 8 7 6 5 4 3 2 1

To Andrea Stevens, whose choice led me to the world of Choose Your Own Adventure *in the first place. Much gratitude!*

BEWARE and WARNING!

This book is different from other books.

You and YOU ALONE are in charge of what happens in this story.

There are dangers, choices, adventures and consequences. YOU must use all of your numerous talents and much of your enormous intelligence. The wrong decision could end in disaster—even death. But don't despair. At any time, YOU can go back and make another choice, alter the path of your story, and change its result.

After a unicorn rescue mission brought you from your home in Flanders to Scotland, you're finally settling into your new life. You spend your days working as an apprentice to the brilliant Dame Scotia, who uses her magic to turn cats into pegacorns (flying unicorns)! Except, one day you arrive home and discover that Dame Scotia is missing. Is she in danger? Only YOU can track her down and save her pegacorns from a terrible fate!

If flying the new pegacorn, Liss, hadn't been so thrilling, maybe you would have returned in time to prevent all the trouble in the first place. But you didn't. It was just too exhilarating to soar over the mountains and castles of Scotland. Taking brand-new winged unicorns on their first flight is the best part of your job, and each time you take to the sky, you fly higher and farther.

Today, you've gone beyond Edinburgh. As you circle back to the harbor, seagulls glide by, eyeing you with curiosity. You remember how curious you felt a year ago, in 1510, when you first arrived to rescue a unicorn taken from your homeland of Flanders. You've learned so much since then—not just the language, but even something about magic, thanks to Dame Scotia, who hired you as her assistant. Now you live with her and her many white cats while she teaches you how to help the magic unfold!

In Scotland, it's said that unicorns are as common as cats. That's a bit of an exaggeration, but they aren't nearly as rare as they are in Flanders. The ones that freely roam the Scottish Highlands have always been unicorns, but many others started their lives as white cats before Dame Scotia transformed them into green-eyed unicorns. The Scots treasure their unicorns. A rich lord might keep a unicorn or two as a prized pet, but no one would think of hurting one.

Turn to page 3.

Hardly anyone has ever seen a flying unicorn, known as a pegacorn, however. The only pegacorns that exist are the ones Dame Scotia has been creating with your help. She has the magic, and you have the excellent sewing skills needed to make their wings. You also take the pegacorns on their first flights, just as you are doing right now.

You suddenly realize that you've probably made this first flight too long. The new pegacorn, Liss, is showing signs of exhaustion. Strangely, it's almost as if your own shoulders have become weary and your own bones ache in sympathy with his. Even though this pegacorn is just a couple of hours old, you already feel deeply connected to him. You turn toward Dame Scotia's house to descend.

Landing a pegacorn is always tricky the first time. Liss stumbles awkwardly as his hooves touch the earth, but he catches his balance. His green eyes sparkle with pride. "You were amazing!" you tell him, stroking his mane, and you realize your own life in Edinburgh is amazing too. You lead Liss into the stable and give him some water. "I think you might be my favorite pegacorn ever!" you whisper. You wonder when you will be able to fly with him again.

As you step outside the stable, you notice that Dame Scotia is nowhere to be seen. She usually watches the landing closely. You must have been gone a really long time! Several of her white cats come over to wind themselves around your legs, and you sense that they are not just being friendly. They seem anxious.

Turn to the next page.

4

You pick up the largest cat, nuzzle her face, and say, "Eleanor, what's wrong?" Even though Eleanor has some remarkable skills, speaking is not one of them, so you don't really expect an answer. The other cats scurry to the front door, and you notice it is partially open.

"I'm back!" you call as you enter the house. You are stunned! White feathers are scattered everywhere, and the table where you sew has been overturned. Dame Scotia's bed is a tangle of linens. "Dame Scotia?" you call as your heart starts to pound. A flash of silver on the floor catches your eye. When you reach for it, you realize it's one of the stars from her red curls. Dame Scotia uses these stars in her magic spells and she doesn't let them drop casually from her hair. Either she was taken violently or she intentionally let them fall to signal you.

You run upstairs to the loft where you sleep. Everything has been overturned there as well, but there's no sign of Dame Scotia. You have to find her! Without her, you really have no life in Scotland.

"Dame Scotia? Dame Scotia!" you shout.

It's clear that Dame Scotia didn't leave by choice. She would have waited for your return to say goodbye and told you where she was going. What's more, she wouldn't have emptied baskets of feathers and turned furniture upside down. You try to think who would have kidnapped her. As far as you can tell, Dame Scotia has no enemies.

Go on to the next page.

Suddenly, you remember her telling you about an unwelcome visit a few weeks ago from Lord Padraig, one of the most powerful men in Scotland. First, he offered to buy pegacorns, but Dame Scotia refused. She always lets the pegacorns she creates fly free.

Then he offered to hire her to transform the unicorns he already owns into pegacorns. Lord Padraig wanted to create an army of flying unicorns so he could take over all of Scotland, and maybe eventually beyond!

Dame Scotia and you were horrified at the thought of using pegacorns for war. No matter how much Lord Padraig offered, Dame Scotia refused. He left angrily and insisted he would have his flying army one way or another. You feel certain he is behind Dame Scotia's disappearance.

You have to start searching for Dame Scotia immediately! In your room, you sort through the mess for a few things to take on your journey. As you pull clothes out of a small chest, you hear the door to the house open. Your heart skips a beat. Could it be Dame Scotia returning, or is it someone else?

If you climb into the chest to hide,
turn to page 7.

If you try to sneak downstairs for a look,
turn to page 12.

As quietly as you can, you squeeze into the wooden chest. You can't lower the lid completely, so you pull some bed linens over the top. You can hear someone moving on the floor below you, and then the stairs creak as someone comes up. You hold your breath and try to freeze every muscle in your body. Footsteps enter the room and shuffle around, and just when you think your lungs will explode, the person leaves and walks downstairs.

You take huge gulps of air. You are positive that if that person had been Dame Scotia, she would have called your name. Good thing you hid!

After what feels like an hour, long after you stopped hearing movement below, you climb out of the chest. You go downstairs, where the cats are circling the room, still waiting to be fed. You give each of them a dried fish and help yourself to an oatcake.

The cats follow you outside to look for evidence of Dame Scotia's departure. The smallest kitten, Yan, noses a small star lying on the threshold. You look up and down the road, but don't see any clue.

Turn to page 9.

Even though you're not sure where to begin your search, you know it will be easier if you have a pegacorn for flight. You and the cats head toward the stable. Your heart starts beating faster when you see that the door isn't fully latched. You *know* you closed it properly this morning. Worse yet— Liss is gone! Whoever came into the house must have stolen the pegacorn!

You pick up Eleanor and bury your face in her fur. "This is getting worse and worse! I don't know where to start!" you cry. Eleanor wriggles out of your arms and jumps to the ground. With a quick flick of her tail, she saunters down the lane. You know she is an excellent tracker, so without a second thought, you follow her.

As ridiculous as it is to follow a cat, this isn't the first time Eleanor has led you to someone useful. You try to act nonchalant, as if you are just out for a morning stroll and the large white cat prancing a few feet ahead of you is of no interest whatsoever.

Reaching the center of town, you meet Hendon sitting outside the church. Hendon is generally regarded as the fool of Edinburgh. His tunic is patched with bright bits of silk and velvet. *Where does he even get luxurious scraps like those?* you wonder. He doesn't always make sense, and yet he talks to everyone and seems to know *everything* that is happening. Could that be why Eleanor led you to him?

Turn to the next page.

Eleanor leaps into his lap and he strokes her with affection. "I love this cat!" he exclaims.

"Have you seen Dame Scotia?" You try to sound casual, but you can hear the urgency in your own voice.

Hendon rolls his head from side to side. "Haven't *exactly* seen her today, but I do have an idea about where she's gone."

"Oh tell me! Tell me!" you cry.

Hendon hugs Eleanor tightly. She licks his cheek. "Nothing is free," he says. "How do you think I ended up with these beautiful scraps?" He sticks out his feet and admires his surprisingly fine shoes. "Or these shoes? There's a cost to my secrets."

Go on to the next page.

"Hendon," you reply, "I'm sure you have valuable information, but I have nothing to trade. I'm Dame Scotia's assistant, but she doesn't really pay me. Please tell me, and when Dame Scotia comes back, I'm sure she will give you something wonderful, maybe even a unicorn."

Hendon rolls his eyes. "What would I do with a unicorn? No, what I want is one cat. *This* cat, Eleanor."

"Not Eleanor!" you cry. "We have many cats. You can choose any of them, but Eleanor is Dame Scotia's favorite. My favorite too! She would kill me if I let you have Eleanor."

Hendon smiles slyly. "I don't think you will ever see Dame Scotia again without my help."

You notice Eleanor is now purring loudly and licking Hendon's hand. Maybe she would be very happy with him. She's certainly clever enough to escape if she wants to. But how will *you* ever find Dame Scotia without Eleanor's help?

If you agree to trade Eleanor for information about Dame Scotia and the pegacorn, turn to page 21.

If you refuse to trade Eleanor, turn to page 26.

12

As quietly as you can, you gently tiptoe until you can sneak a look down from the top of the stairs. You see the back of a woman with long curls and call out, "Dame Scotia! You're back!"

She turns to you as you run down the stairs and fling your arms around her. The woman gently pries you off and holds you at arm's length. "You must be my sister's assistant," she says with a smile.

At first, you are too shocked and disappointed to answer. Now you see that her hair is not the brilliant red of Dame Scotia's. Her dress isn't as bright either. Like her hair, it's the color of a fox. Instead of stars sparkling in her curls, here and there, tiny crescent moons catch the light.

"I didn't know Dame Scotia had a sister," you finally say.

Turn to page 14.

"We haven't seen each other in a while," says the woman. "She may not have mentioned me. I'm Dame Tira."

"She's gone! Do you have any idea where she could be?" you ask. You are suddenly grateful to have someone who can help you find Dame Scotia.

Go on to the next page.

"Yes," says Dame Tira calmly. "In fact, I've come to bring you and the pegacorn to her."

Now you're confused. Maybe Lord Padraig didn't kidnap Dame Scotia? But why didn't Dame Scotia take you and Liss in the first place? And why does it look like a struggle took place?

"Where is she? Why would she leave me here?"

"So many questions," sighs Dame Tira. "There's no need for you to worry, but we really must hurry. Show me the pegacorn." With one hand still on your shoulder, she propels you out the door, even though you aren't sure you willed your feet to move.

Turn to the next page.

16

As you swing the stable door open, all five cats rush in as well. You notice Dame Tira tries to step away from them.

"Are you afraid of cats?" you ask.

"Of course not," she scoffs. "I just don't like the smell of dead rats on their breath."

Dame Scotia feeds her cats so well that you are pretty sure they have never eaten rats.

Little Yan noses under the woman's skirt and she kicks the kitten away. "Get these creatures out of here!" she snaps.

You shoo the cats out of the stable, then follow them outside. You are about to return to the stable when you decide to pick up Yan and put her inside your pocket. It's always good to travel with a cat!

Go on to the next page.

When you return inside the stable, Dame Tira is tugging the tired pegacorn's horn.

"You aren't thinking we will fly on Liss, are you?" you ask. "He just made his first flight, and it was a long one. It's really too soon for him to fly again, especially with two people on his back. Let me go get another from the paddock."

"There's no time—my sister needs you," Dame Tira says. "This pegacorn is going to have to do his best."

"Then I think I had better be the one in front with the reins," you say as you put a bridle on Liss.

Turn to the next page.

18

The two of you climb onto the pegacorn, and Dame Tira puts her arms around your waist. Liss moves awkwardly. Even when he takes to the air, he flies low enough that you have to watch out for tree branches.

"Where are we going?" you ask.

"Head west. We need to find Lord Padraig's castle."

"I *thought* he might have been the one to kidnap her!" you exclaim as you guide Liss away from a low-hanging bough. "We're going to rescue Dame Scotia, aren't we?"

"Not exactly," Dame Tira replies. "You and the pegacorn were supposed to have gone with her."

"Why does he want *me*?"

"Don't flatter yourself," says Dame Tira. "He wants whoever sews the wings my sister needs to create flying unicorns. He has plans for a flying army that will soar too high for the arrows of his enemies."

You frown. "That's a terrible use of pegacorns! Your sister isn't going to like this idea at all."

Turn to page 20.

20

Dame Tira snorts in a most unladylike manner. "Of course she won't. Now *see* if you can get this animal to fly faster!"

You feel a wriggling in your pocket and remember Yan is tucked in there. You watch the kitten crawl out over your thigh and around your hip, wedging herself between you and Dame Tira.

Dame Tira's scream is deafening! She lets go of your waist as she tries to push away the kitten, and you realize that if you fly through the elm branches nearby, you could knock her off Liss's back. But should you? She *is* Dame Scotia's sister, and besides, how will you find Lord Padraig's castle without her?

If you decide to fly through the elm branches to dislodge Dame Tira, turn to page 31.

If you decide you'd better continue on with her, turn to page 54.

As much as you hate the idea of giving Eleanor to Hendon, you do really need his help in finding Dame Scotia. "Okay," you say reluctantly. "You can have Eleanor. I think she likes you better than she likes me anyway. Tell me where Dame Scotia is!"

Hendon nuzzles Eleanor. "I don't know exactly where she is. . . ."

"Hendon!" you shriek. "You said you had information!" You have a sinking feeling that this may have been a very bad trade.

He smiles coyly. "I know that some fancy-shmancy lord has been asking about the magic she uses to create pegacorns. He wants them for war!"

"Lord Padraig?"

"Exactly. Now that I think of it, he's the same one who imported that Flemish unicorn last year."

Turn to the next page.

22

You can't believe your ears! That's the unicorn that led you to Scotland in the first place! If only you had known then that it was Lord Padraig who had the unicorn, you could have rescued it by now! You think back to Dame Scotia's account of Lord Padraig's visit, but can't recall any mention of the Flemish unicorn.

Eleanor is curled up quite comfortably in Hendon's lap. You can even hear her purring.

"Do you think Lord Padraig kidnapped Dame Scotia?"

"Not Lord Padraig himself, of course. He has many people working for him. Just about an hour ago, I saw a very ornate carriage heading out of Edinburgh on the western road. Such a fine carriage could only belong to one of the richest lords."

Go on to the next page.

"Did you see Dame Scotia in the carriage?"

"I didn't have such a clear view," he admits. "In fact, I couldn't even make out the coat of arms on the side."

"Where is Lord Padraig's castle?"

Hendon nuzzles Eleanor again. "I can't believe you're my cat now," he murmurs to her.

"Hendon!"

"Somewhere west of Edinburgh, along the river. You know I've never left the city myself."

As you start to walk away, you wonder if the information you gained was really worth the loss of Eleanor. You decide to squeeze a little more out of Hendon and turn back.

"One more thing," you say. "Our pegacorn was stolen this morning too. Do you know anything about that?"

Hendon laughs. "Well, that explains what I saw shortly before you came. Dame Scotia's sister fell from the sky, from a pegacorn!"

"Dame Scotia has a sister? How come I never knew about that?"

He rolls his eyes again. "There is so much you don't know. If I were you, I'd go back home and see if your pegacorn has returned."

Turn to the next page.

You quickly thank Hendon and hurry home, where you find the stable door still open, and Liss inside, munching hay as if he had never been stolen. "Oh Liss, I'm so happy to see you!" You wrap your arms around his neck and he whinnies with pleasure.

You decide to leave immediately. You remember Dame Scotia's saying, "A cat for the road brightens your load." The first time you heard it, you thought she said "lightens the load," and were confused because cats, of course, can't carry parcels. "No, no," she clarified. "Brightens! A cat makes everything more vivid!" For a moment, you wish you could take Eleanor, the excellent tracker, but then you remember she is no longer yours, so you pick up Yan, the smallest kitten, who fits right in your pocket. You climb on Liss, and his wings carry you into the air. You notice he's flying with effort, and feel bad that he didn't have a longer rest. However, you *do* have to rescue Dame Scotia!

Go on to the next page.

Checking the sun for direction, you guide Liss to the road leading west from Edinburgh. It's a beautiful morning for flying—not too windy, and the sky is clear. Every now and then, you fly over a flock of sheep on the road, or someone on horseback. You swoop closer to check out a wagon but can see it's empty. Finally, you spot a carriage led by four strong horses. Only a lord could afford this luxury!

Now that you've spotted the carriage that might be holding Dame Scotia, you realize you're not sure what to do next! You could land in front of the carriage and force them to stop, or you could fly farther ahead and land where you can hide.

If you swoop down to force the carriage to stop, turn to page 36.

If you fly past the carriage, turn to page 38.

"Hendon, I'm sorry, but I can't trade Eleanor." As you take Eleanor from his arms, you can't help noticing that the cat is eyeing Hendon longingly.

"Do you think Lord Padraig kidnapped her?" you ask before you leave him. "He visited her a while ago and wanted pegacorns for a flying army."

Hendon shrugs with indifference. "Seems possible." You can tell he isn't going to give you any help without Eleanor!

"Also, have you seen our newest pegacorn? He was stolen this morning."

"Hmmmm," says Hendon. "I would remember these things so much more clearly if I had Eleanor."

"Forget about it, Hendon. I'm not giving you Eleanor." You shift the cat to your other arm and start to walk away.

You take only a few steps before you realize you have no idea where to begin to look.

"Hendon, please," you say, "can you just tell me where Lord Padraig's castle is?"

Go on to the next page.

Hendon doesn't answer for a few frustrating moments. Finally, he says, "I have never been his guest, but I'm told it's to the west along the river. It will be a very, very long walk."

That gives you an idea! If the castle is near the River Forth, you could try to take a boat there! Clutching Eleanor, you hurry over to the harbor to see what boats are sailing in that direction.

As you go from boat to boat to inquire, someone grabs your shoulder and turns you around. Your heart skips a beat, until you recognize who it is.

"Captain Hullett!" you exclaim. "I haven't seen you since I came to Edinburgh on your ship!"

"I thought that was you," he said warmly. "I recall you came to Scotland to rescue a unicorn, but I see that you've ended up with a cat instead."

"It's a long story."

"Well, then come on board for some food and tell me," Captain Hullett proposes.

When you were a cook on Captain Hullett's ship, you ate with the rest of the sailors, never in his private room. It's strange to have someone else bring you food, but you're ravenous, and grateful for the meal. Between bites, you tell him everything that's happened, right up to your search for Dame Scotia.

Turn to the next page.

"Lord Padraig is a rich and dangerous man," says Captain Hullett, "so you are going to need powerful help. Luckily, I've met the Archbishop of St. Andrews. Tomorrow, we are sailing there to deliver some goods to him. He's a nice young man who even speaks some Flemish. I could try to introduce you. I'm sure he would do everything possible to stop the creation of a pegacorn army."

"That sounds great!"

"On the other hand," he continues, "the King is at Edinburgh Castle right now to celebrate the completion of the Great Hall. I know this because we delivered all kinds of supplies for a banquet he is having tonight. Of course, I'm not acquainted with the King, but I think you are spunky enough to slip in among his guests. If you could get his attention, I'm sure he would launch an army to oppose Lord Padraig."

Two excellent ideas! Captain Hullett's personal connection to the Archbishop would be helpful, but it will take longer to sail to his location. It would be faster to sneak into Edinburgh Castle tonight, but would you really be able to get the ear of the King? You're not even Scottish!

If you decide to go to St. Andrews with Captain Hullett, turn to page 41.

If you decide to try to meet the King tonight, turn to page 65.

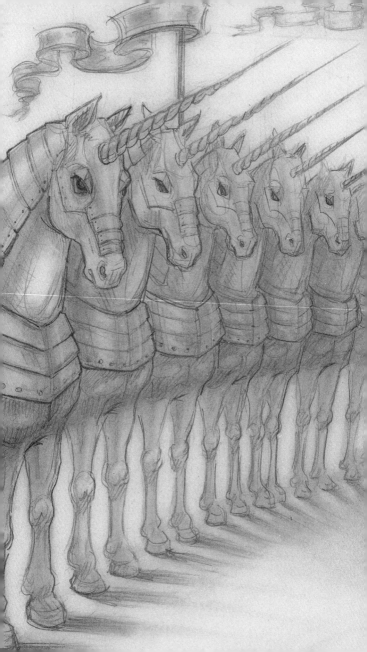

While Dame Tira flails her arms with fear, you direct Liss toward a nearby elm tree and fly straight into the branches. Sure enough, Dame Tira is knocked off, and you leave her clutching a bough and screeching with rage.

You fly Liss until you are just outside the city walls. By the time you land, Liss is shaking with exhaustion. You let him rest, and then slowly lead him on foot down the western road while Yan scampers ahead. Whenever you come to someone, you ask about Lord Padraig's castle. Everyone says it's in the west, but no one has ever actually been there.

You finally see the castle with a blue unicorn flag flying from each of its four towers. Away from the castle, you tie Liss to a tree near a stream. The last thing you want is for Lord Padraig to seize this pegacorn for his army!

Turn to the next page.

You are tired and dirty when you approach the guards. So much travel has taken its toll. You place Yan in your pocket with a warning to be still.

"I'm a starving orphan," you tell them. "Please, can I be a servant for Lord Padraig? I'm especially good with a needle, but I will do any work that is needed."

One of the guards leads you into the castle. You look around with awe, wondering what it must be like to live in these large rooms with elaborately carved furniture.

"A lady arrived earlier today," the guard tells you, "and she would probably be happy to have you mend her clothing."

Your heart leaps with excitement. "Is her name Dame Scotia?"

The guard eyes you with curiosity. "For a poor orphan, you seem to know a lot of people. No, the lady I was speaking of is—oh, right here!"

Go on to the next page.

Dame Tira, Dame Scotia's sister, is striding down the hall!

"What are you doing here?" you ask with shock and horror.

"You mean why am I not dead?"

You decide not to answer that question.

"Actually, I'm glad you're here. I need you to sew wings," says Dame Tira.

"Where is Dame Scotia?" you ask.

"She's here," says Dame Tira, "but she's not cooperating, and as a result, she's not doing well."

"I'm not doing anything until I talk to her," you insist.

Dame Tira takes your arm and pulls you into the castle, where you meet Lord Padraig for the first time. He's a handsome man with cruel eyes.

"Ah, Dame Scotia's assistant!" he exclaims. "Wonderful! Let me show you what happens to people who do not cooperate with me."

Turn to page 35.

The three of you head down a dark and winding staircase to the dungeon. Spiderwebs drape every corner and rats scurry by without a trace of fear. It's dark and dank, and already you are scared. In one corner, your eyes make out a huddled figure who is so filthy, so bedraggled, and so ill that you can barely recognize Dame Scotia. You have to fight back tears.

When her eyes meet yours, they are expressionless. You're not even sure she recognizes you.

"You can join her in the dungeon," says Lord Padraig, "or you can sew wings for a pegacorn."

"Don't," whispers Dame Scotia weakly.

"In fact, for each pair of wings you sew, we will bring her a meal, maybe even some herbs to help her recover," says Lord Padraig.

You are torn. Of course you want to obey Dame Scotia, but she is clearly dying. Besides, if she won't use her magic to transform unicorns into pegacorns, it doesn't really matter if you make wings or not. Can you let her die?

If you decide to obey Dame Scotia's words and refuse to sew wings, turn to page 74.

If you agree to sew wings, turn to page 78.

36

You guide Liss down about twenty paces in front of the horses. The carriage driver pulls the reins to stop and then shouts, "Out of the way!"

You dismount, leaving Liss to block the road, and hurry over to the carriage. Inside, you see Dame Scotia with her arms tied, and a guard beside her.

As soon as she sees you, she yells, "Leave! Leave right now! This is not safe!"

"I've come to rescue you!"

Dame Scotia tosses her head toward the man beside her. "You can't! Save yourself!"

You have only seconds to decide! Should you climb back on the pegacorn and take to the air, or stay to help Dame Scotia?

If you obey and race back to Liss to escape, turn to page 45.

If you insist on staying to rescue Dame Scotia, turn to page 50.

You fly until the road crosses a small stream. You know that Liss needs water, and it's possible the horses drawing the carriage will too. If the carriage stops, you'll be able to see if Dame Scotia is inside.

Liss eagerly laps at the stream. You run your fingers through his mane and tell him how strong he is. Then the two of you wander along the stream until you meet an older woman dressed entirely in green.

"Good day, young one!" she greets you, but it's the pegacorn she's looking at. You drape your arm over Liss protectively and smooth the feathers on his wings.

"Good day to you too," you reply, and nod your head respectfully. As your eyes lower, you catch sight of her webbed feet! You start to feel uneasy. Dame Scotia once warned you about someone like this.

"Good dame, may I ask your name?" you inquire as politely as you can manage.

The woman smiles broadly, revealing her missing teeth. "I'm known as Bean Nighe."

Your heart stops! Dame Scotia swore that Bean Nighe is an omen of death!

Turn to page 40.

40

You are too terrified to respond. You nod your head nervously.

"I know why you're frightened," says Bean Nighe, "but you needn't be. Trade me that winged unicorn and I will give you three wishes. Otherwise, yes, you will meet death before the sun sets."

You drop to your knees with relief. This is not a hard decision!

"My first wish is to be safely back in Edinburgh with Dame Scotia."

You wait. Nothing happens.

"Go on," says Bean Nighe. "I want to hear them all."

You take a deep breath. "I want Lord Padraig to forget all about war. And lastly, I want Liss to be very happy with you."

Bean Nighe smiles. "Granted!"

In a flash, Dame Scotia is gently waking you. "Where am I?" you ask.

"Right here in your bed in Edinburgh, silly! But I'm afraid I have some bad news. Liss is missing from the stable!"

You sink back to your pillow with relief. "That's not such bad news. I think Liss will be happy wherever he is. What about Yan? Where's our smallest kitten?"

Dame Scotia looks around uneasily. "Hmmm. Now that you mention it, I haven't seen . . ."

At just that second you feel wriggling in the bed beside you, and Yan pokes her tiny white ears out of the covers.

The End

"I'm not sure I can really talk to the King," you tell Captain Hullett. "If you can introduce me to the Archbishop, I think he would listen to me."

"I'm happy to have you and your cat on board!" he replies.

The next morning, the voyage to St. Andrews begins. Eleanor roams the ship, chasing rats, while you stay on deck, watching the rugged coast of Scotland as it passes.

St. Andrews is a much smaller town than Edinburgh, and Captain Hullett's ship is greeted with great excitement. There are a few small fishing boats, but no other merchant ships. You cuddle Eleanor while you wait for the Archbishop's goods to be loaded on carts. Then you, Captain Hullett, and Eleanor follow them to the church.

There are servants to receive the crates. "I'd like to see the Archbishop," Captain Hullett announces.

"You'll have to sail back to Edinburgh to see him," a servant replies. "He's there to celebrate the opening of the Great Hall!"

You can't believe your bad luck!

Turn to the next page

42

Captain Hullett flushes with embarrassment. "I'm sorry," he tells you, "but I don't know the Archbishop's social schedule."

You try to conceal your disappointment. "That's okay. I can sail back to Edinburgh with you."

Captain Hullett shakes his head. "I'm afraid you can't. I'm continuing north. I can't turn the ship around to take you back." You recall that the harbor of St. Andrews had only fishing boats, not the kind that could take you back to Edinburgh.

"When will the Archbishop return?" you ask the servant.

"I imagine as soon as he possibly can. He won't want to be away from his new baby unicorn for very long." The servant points to a tiny unicorn curled in a corner.

You've never seen such a young unicorn! Many dogs are bigger than this sweet creature! Everything about it seems to glow. The baby unicorn gazes at you with curiosity.

You pick up the unicorn and hold it over your shoulder as if it were an infant. It smells remarkably like a human baby. Eleanor rubs against your legs, and you know she is jealous.

Turn to page 44.

44

"I will wait," you announce, "and maybe I can take care of this baby unicorn in the meantime."

"I'm sorry to disappoint you twice," says Captain Hullett, "but I don't think you will succeed in rescuing Dame Scotia. There's not enough time. The King's festivities will continue for several days, and when the Archbishop finally returns, he is not going to turn around again to tell the King about Lord Padraig's plan. I can't stay to introduce you, so he may not even agree to talk to you. Come back to the ship with me and join my crew. You were the best cook we ever had. You can see other unicorns on our travels."

Even with the baby unicorn nuzzling your ear, making it hard to concentrate, you realize that Captain Hullett is probably right. You could stay and enjoy being with the baby unicorn until the Archbishop returns. Then you could try to get him to listen to you. On the other hand, a life of adventure on Captain Hullett's boat sounds very exciting!

If you decide to wait with the baby unicorn for the Archbishop, turn to page 107.

If you decide to join Captain Hullett's crew, turn to page 82.

You decide to heed Dame Scotia's warning, and you dash back to the pegacorn. The carriage driver is right behind you, but before he can catch you, Liss carries you into the air. Even though the pegacorn must be tired, he is doing his best to protect you.

You circle the carriage from above and decide to follow it. At first, it's easy to keep up. You soar over villages, flocks of sheep, and stony hills, always with the River Forth to your right. However, the longer you fly, the weaker Liss becomes. You remind yourself this is his first day in the air, and already he's gone very far!

You're looking below for a good place for Liss to rest when you notice a white blur of animals in a meadow to the south. The animals are too bright to be sheep, and . . . are those horns? You swoop lower for a closer look. Sure enough, there are more unicorns than you can count, surely two dozen, but maybe three.

Turn page 47.

You land Liss beside the herd of grazing unicorns. They lift their heads and whinny with surprise. A few come over to sniff Liss's wings. You walk into the middle of the herd and nuzzle their heads, running your hand up and down their horns. They're very friendly!

Yan jumps out of your pocket and scampers around the unicorns until she comes to one with eyes as green as Liss's. She licks its hoof affectionately. All the unicorns and pegacorns that Dame Scotia creates have the same emerald eyes, so you know this unicorn must have been one of Yan's relatives in Dame Scotia's home. That reminds you—you don't have all day to pet unicorns. You need to rescue Dame Scotia!

Liss is clearly too tired to resume flying, but you pick up Yan and climb on the green-eyed unicorn. As you start to ride toward the road, you realize the dozens of unicorns are following you! Even Liss is following on foot.

After a few more hours of riding, you reach a castle flying unicorn flags from each of its four towers. You feel certain this must be Lord Padraig's. Although there are guards, they are so surprised by the vast herd of unicorns that they let you through the gate and follow you past the wall with wonder. You ride around the outside of the castle to a fenced paddock, where about a dozen unicorns turn their heads to greet you.

Standing among them is a red-haired woman. "Dame Scotia!" you call out.

Turn to the next page.

48

Dame Scotia hurries toward the paddock gate. You see a finely dressed man dash after her, but another more humbly dressed man pulls him back. Dame Scotia flings open the gate and runs to you.

"I can't believe you're here! We must escape!" she exclaims. She climbs onto a unicorn, motions to the others inside the paddock, and says, "Let's go!" You both race away from the paddock, with the rest of the unicorns following close behind.

The castle guards mount their horses and begin chasing you, but the herd of unicorns protects you. They're galloping faster than the horses, faster than the barking dogs that run behind you. Arrows shoot past, so you duck your head and hold onto the unicorn's neck as tightly as you can. You race along a winding hillside path so narrow that two unicorns barely fit side by side.

Dame Scotia abruptly stops and says, "No." All the unicorns stop too. She carefully turns her unicorn around, and so do you. "No," she says again. "*We* are attacking *them*!"

Go on to the next page.

Every unicorn turns to face the men. You and Dame Scotia are now at the tail end of the stampede galloping toward the men on horses. You can't even see what is happening, but you hear a scream and see a horse tumbling into the valley far below.

The unicorns lower their horns like swords and race toward the horses. There's bright blood, and more horses plunge off the path with riders flailing their arms in panic. You've never seen unicorns fight before, but they are fierce! Finally, the last of Lord Padraig's men turn around and gallop away.

The herd of unicorns stops, carefully turns around, and slowly resumes walking away from Lord Padraig's castle.

"I didn't know unicorns could do that," you tell Dame Scotia once you catch your breath.

"There's a lot more for you to learn about unicorns when we get home," she replies.

The End

50

You start to tell Dame Scotia that you are determined to stay with her, but before the words leave your mouth, the driver seizes you from behind. The guard beside Dame Scotia jumps out of the carriage to help tie your hands behind your back.

"Tie up the unicorn! I've got this one!" he snarls to the driver. But it's too late. Liss has already taken flight. It's the only thing you feel happy about at the moment.

The guard and the driver load you into the carriage beside Dame Scotia. The guard sits across from you, gloating. "The lord is going to be pleased about this!" he says.

"What happened?" you ask Dame Scotia.

"Shhhh! We can't talk here!" says Dame Scotia.

You nod to show you understand. As the carriage rocks along the bumpy road, the rope cuts painfully into your arms. Soon you are desperately thirsty. You watch the guard yawn, and before long he drifts into sleep.

Go on to the next page.

You turn to Dame Scotia to speak, but she shakes her head. On your thigh, you feel a movement, and are startled to see Yan's little white head emerge from your pocket. You had completely forgotten she was with you! Dame Scotia notices Yan too, smiles with surprised delight, and begins making very soft cooing noises to her. Yan climbs up to Dame Scotia's shoulder, nestling in her long curls. Dame Scotia gently tosses her head until her hair completely conceals the kitten. After what feels like forever, the carriage stops by the river so the horses can drink.

"We would like to drink some water too, please," says Dame Scotia.

Turn to the next page.

52

The guard helps the two of you down from the carriage and brings a cup of water first to Dame Scotia's face, and then to yours.

"That was wonderful! Thank you!" she tells the guard graciously. "Now, would it be possible to go behind those trees to relieve myself?"

"One at a time," says the guard. "You're going first."

Dame Scotia again smiles at him and says, "You are so kind. Thank you. However, I will need my hands free to manage my skirt."

"No, you don't," snaps the guard.

"Please, sir," she says. "I am a lady. Allow me to meet Lord Padraig with dignity and not as a prisoner with a wet skirt."

The guard reluctantly unties her hands and Dame Scotia walks toward the woods. You hope the guard didn't notice the brief flick of a small white tail poking out from her hair.

Go on to the next page.

Dame Scotia is gone long enough to make everyone nervous. When she finally returns, she smiles with what appears to be genuine delight and says to you, "Seize the opportunity!" Before the guard reties her hands, she uses them to lift her curls off her shoulders and toss her hair. You see that Yan is no longer hiding there!

"Your turn, and be quick," says the guard as he unties your hands.

You scurry into the woods, looking for a discreet place to pee. You see a large boulder and step behind it, but to your amazement, there's a small unicorn standing there! Its green eyes look at you expectantly.

"Yan?" you whisper. This unicorn's green eyes are a sign that she began life as a cat before being transformed by Dame Scotia.

As the unicorn nuzzles your belly, you remember Dame Scotia urging you to seize the opportunity. Was she telling you to escape? This unicorn is much too small for an adult to ride, and maybe not even big enough to carry you. You insisted on staying with Dame Scotia before, but so far, you haven't been very helpful.

If you quickly climb on the unicorn to flee, turn to page 60.

If you leave the unicorn and return to the carriage, turn to page 62.

54

"Get that cat away from me! Are you trying to kill me?" Dame Tira screeches. You reach back and return Yan to your pocket.

"Where exactly does Lord Padraig live?" you ask.

"I've never been to his castle," Dame Tira admits. "It's west of Edinburgh, but let's stop whenever we see one. What's that on the hill over there?"

You can see that Liss is shaking from the exhaustion of carrying two people, so you are happy to guide him toward the castle. You lead Liss to a drawbridge over the moat. Two guards stand there, watching you approach.

"Good morning!" you say. "My pegacorn needs water."

"And I'd like to speak with your lord," adds Dame Tira.

One of the guards takes Liss's reins, and you hesitate to release them. "I'll take good care of your winged unicorn," he says, and finally you let go.

The other guard leads you to a great chamber hung with tapestries. One of them shows a unicorn surrounded by a fence. You are looking at that closely when you hear an entourage enter the hall.

Turn to page 56.

56

"Oh, Lord Eòsaph," Dame Tira exclaims. "I had no idea this was your home."

"Welcome, welcome!" he says and kisses her hand. "Please, stay for dinner!"

You can see Dame Tira is uncertain. "Well, Lord Padraig is expecting us, but I suppose we could arrive tomorrow."

You tug her arm and say, "But what about Dame Scotia?"

Dame Tira waves you off dismissively. "Yes, it's been a harrowing journey and I'm quite weary. Thank you for your hospitality, Lord Eòsaph!"

Go on to the next page.

Lord Eòsaph places his hand on Dame Tira's back and leans his head toward hers. "Why would you want to visit Padraig?"

Dame Tira smiles coyly. "My sister is with him. I need to deliver a flying unicorn and this servant to them."

Lord Eòsaph's eyebrows shoot up.

Before he can say a word, you tell him, "Lord Padraig wants to have an army of flying unicorns."

Dame Tira shushes you immediately. "The servant speaks nonsense," she assures Lord Eòsaph, but he is looking at you with curiosity.

"Will you help him?" he asks.

"Not me!" you answer. "She's the one who's helping Lord Padraig!"

"Not anymore!" he laughs. "If Padraig has a flying army, his first attack will be right here! I'm afraid I can't let you go."

Dame Tira stamps her foot and glares at you.

"What about me?" you ask.

"Do as you wish," he replies, "but I could send my best spy with you to retrieve Dame Scotia and steal a unicorn or two from his collection for me."

"Thank you! I would welcome some help!"

Turn to the next page.

58

You spend the night in Lord Eòsaph's castle. You had hoped to be served as a guest, but end up eating with the servants. Even if the food is unremarkable, it's plentiful, and you manage to swipe a bit of fish for Yan. You and the kitten curl up in the servants' quarters, and you both fall asleep almost immediately. The next morning before the sun has even risen, a teenaged girl who appears to be a servant wakes you.

"There's food in this pouch to eat on the way. Let's go!" she whispers.

"What's going on? Who are you?"

"I'm Susannah. We need to get an early start to reach Lord Padraig's castle by breakfast." She is pulling you out of bed.

"You're Lord Eòsaph's best spy?"

"I am!"

You are skeptical. This girl is just a couple of years older than you. In the candlelight, you can see that her clothes are patched and tattered, not what you expect Lord Eòsaph's best spy to wear. She turns her head and you spot a tiny silver moon in her uncombed hair. It's just like the ones in Dame Tira's curls. What if she is working for Dame Tira to prevent you from rescuing Dame Scotia?

If you decide to trust her, turn to page 83.

If you decide to slip out of the castle without her, turn to page 110.

You swing your leg over Yan's back and find your feet almost touch the ground. You feel bad that Yan's first moments as a unicorn will require carrying you. It won't be easy for such a small animal. You ride quickly, but quietly, deeper into the woods so the guard won't find you. You wonder how much time they'll give you to pee before chasing into the woods to look for you.

You try to stay parallel to the road, but before long, you're lost. What's more, Yan is too exhausted to continue carrying you. You dismount and together you walk, trying to find the road but staying clear of the carriage and the guard.

As you trudge through bogs and over hills, sometimes your stomach rumbles with hunger. You remember feeding Yan a small fish this morning when she was still a kitten, but she hasn't eaten anything at all as a unicorn. This is an arduous journey for her too.

Go on to the next page.

As soon as you come to a grassy meadow, you pause so Yan can graze. The unicorn looks at you as if she doesn't understand why you've stopped. You point to the grass and pretend to chew. Is it possible Yan doesn't know how to eat as a unicorn? You guide her head to the ground. She sniffs the grass and looks back up at you. Finally, you pull up some grass and offer it to Yan with your hand. She nibbles tentatively, and then enthusiastically.

Once Yan has gotten used to eating grass by herself, you go off to look for berries. You scramble over rocks, hoping to find some growing in a sunny patch. You're ravenous now, but still can't find anything to eat. Wandering farther away from Yan, you come to several high boulders and what could be the mouth of a cave. You know berries don't grow in caves, so there is no reason to explore that.

Suddenly, a piercing scream makes your heart skip a beat! What *was* that?

If you race back to Yan, turn to page 89.

If you dash into the cave to hide, turn to page 90.

62

Dame Scotia's face fills with disappointment as you emerge from the woods. "What did I tell you?" she asks. It's the first time you've heard anger in her voice.

You shrug. "I can't leave you."

The guard ties your hands again and helps you into the carriage.

The carriage finally arrives at a grand castle beside a river. A blue flag with a unicorn symbol flies from all four towers. As you and Dame Scotia are carried down from the carriage, she whispers, "Let me do the talking."

Your hands are still being untied when a finely dressed man approaches. "Dame Scotia!" he exclaims. "I hope your journey was not too uncomfortable."

Dame Scotia smiles graciously and replies, "We were treated with nothing but kindness, Lord Padraig. Thank you so much." You look at her with surprise. Your throat is parched again and there are rope marks on your wrists. Every joint in your body was jostled by the bumpy ride. *Why is she acting like this?* you wonder.

The man looks at you for the first time. "And this is?"

You are about to introduce yourself when Dame Scotia replies, "One of my servants, a poor Flemish orphan who barely speaks Scottish, but is very good with unicorns. I believe you have quite a few. Surely you could find a use for this poor orphan."

"I heard it was your assistant who sews the pegacorn wings," says Lord Padraig.

Turn to page 64.

"You seem to know a great deal about my business!" Dame Scotia replies sweetly. "You are correct that I have never learned to sew, but that assistant, I'm afraid, is back in Edinburgh. This orphan can care for animals very well, but has few other skills."

You bristle with indignation! You have always been recognized for your needlework! You start to speak, but Dame Scotia shoots you a stern look.

"Unfortunately," she continues, "without that assistant, I will be completely incapable of turning your unicorns into a flying army."

"That is a shame!" says Lord Padraig. "Until we can find your assistant, you are of no worth to me. You will stay in the dungeon rather than a guest chamber."

Dame Scotia's face turns as white as a unicorn. She is not accustomed to discomfort, never mind suffering. It breaks your heart to imagine her in a dark prison below the castle with rats instead of cats as her companions. Should you disobey and tell Lord Padraig that you are the assistant who sews pegacorn wings?

If you reveal your secret skills to Lord Padraig, turn to page 91.

If you remain silent, turn to page 101.

"I'd love to go with you to St. Andrews sometime," you tell Captain Hullett, "but every minute counts. If there's a chance I could talk to the King tonight, I'm going to try that!"

"If anyone can do it, I suspect it's you," says Captain Hullett with a grin. "However, you are going to have to look quite a bit fancier to get into that party."

"I have time to shorten one of Dame Scotia's dresses," you tell him.

"Good luck! Remember, you are always welcome to sail the seas on my ship, or even go home to Flanders, and you can bring your cat too! Or even a unicorn!"

Turn to the next page.

66

After you say goodbye to Captain Hullett, you and Eleanor hurry back to Dame Scotia's. You look through Dame Scotia's dresses, all ranging from bright scarlet to a deeper crimson, until you find one trimmed with lace. You slip into it with excitement. You've never worn anything nearly as elegant in your entire life! Of course, it's too big for you, but you have the sewing skills to make it fit perfectly.

Even though Dame Scotia always wears her long curls loose, you know that's not proper for a king's banquet. With the red cloth you cut off, you create a stylish coif to cover your hair. There's still cloth left, so you sew a vest for Eleanor to match. At first she resists wearing it, and even scratches your hand, but when she sees the other cats admiring her, she struts around rather smugly. Eleanor looks quite regal in red!

You're not sure when the banquet starts, but you decide to go now to watch the guests enter. You pick up Eleanor and head out the door. Outside, you notice the stable door is open even wider, so you walk over to close it. To your astonishment, Liss is inside!

"Am I crazy?" you ask Eleanor. "Wasn't Liss missing before?" This is the most bizarre day of your life!

Turn to page 68.

Eleanor leaps from your arms right onto Liss's back, and that's when you realize that arriving on a pegacorn will *definitely* get the King's attention! It's not easy to straddle a pegacorn in a fancy dress, but once you're flying, all you feel is exhilaration.

You soar over Edinburgh and circle the castle, high on a hill. Carriages are lined up to enter, and in the courtyard there are already many people. Their jewels sparkle in the sunlight. You decide to land in the courtyard to get everyone's attention.

Turn to page 70.

70

As you descend, you hear the people below gasp with surprise. Very, very few have ever seen a pegacorn before! As soon as you land, a curious crowd surrounds you, buzzing with questions.

You scan the throng of people for the King. Of course, you have no idea what the King looks like, but no one is acting like a king.

"Where is the King?" you ask loudly.

An exquisitely dressed young woman answers, "My husband is in the Great Hall."

She's very young, not much more than twenty, and she smiles at you with bright curiosity. She is not what you expected a queen to be like!

"Please tell me your name, and how you came to have this spectacular creature," she continues. She strokes Liss's mane with admiration, and the pegacorn nuzzles her.

Even though you intended to speak to the King, you can't help telling her your name and adding proudly, "I created this pegacorn with Dame Scotia. I made the wings!"

"Remarkable! And that adorable cat!" says the young Queen. She takes Eleanor from you and rubs her face against Eleanor's. "Come, dismount. I'll take you to my husband." When you are on your feet, she links her arm through yours and smiles at you warmly.

Go on to the next page.

Still surrounded by crowds, you lead Liss through the castle to the recently completed Great Hall. You've never been in such an enormous room! High overhead, wooden beams vault from one wall to another. Swords and armor hang on the walls. You are so fascinated that for a moment, you forget you came to speak to the King.

The Queen introduces you to her husband. He seems more interested in Liss than in you, until you say, "Lord Padraig kidnapped Dame Scotia because he wants to create an army of flying unicorns."

His eyebrows shoot up. "That Padraig! I can't risk that. We will celebrate tonight, and tomorrow I'll send an army to attack him. In fact, I'll ride this winged unicorn myself to the battle."

You hadn't intended to give Liss to the King, but you can hardly refuse, especially if it means he will rescue Dame Scotia. You throw your arms around Liss one last time, then curtsy and say, "Your Highness, the pegacorn is yours."

The Queen tugs your arm. "Come, have something to eat before the dancing starts."

Turn to page 73.

The royal banquet is like nothing you could have imagined! You are too excited to eat! You sit beside the Queen at a table that stretches from one end of the room to the other. There's music like you've never heard, and lively dancing, so different from in Flanders. Jesters juggle golden balls and tumble along the magnificent carpets. Laughter fills the hall. You look down at the beautiful red dress you're wearing and pinch yourself. Are you really here?

"What will you do with your future?" asks the Queen. "I welcome you to live here at the castle. I could use someone as clever as you around here. Also, I'm afraid I've fallen in love with your cat." Eleanor purrs in the Queen's lap.

You can't believe this invitation, but you let your imagination roam. Even if you wouldn't be the one riding Liss, you could join the battle against Lord Padraig. Maybe you would be the one to rescue Dame Scotia! Then you remember Captain Hullett. If you get to the harbor early enough, you could join him on the voyage to St. Andrews. In fact, you could sail the seas as a member of his crew. Now that you've had many adventures in Scotland, it would be exciting to explore more of the world.

If you accept the Queen's invitation to move into the castle, turn to page 106.

If you ask to join the King in battle against Lord Padraig, turn to page 111.

If you want to travel the world with Captain Hullett, turn to page 116.

"I won't sew wings for you," you tell Lord Padraig defiantly.

Without a word, he unlocks the dungeon, grabs your shoulder, and tosses you inside. You land in a heap beside Dame Scotia. As you hear the creak of his key in the padlock, you can't help wondering if you made the right decision.

Dame Scotia puts her arm around you consolingly, and you start to cry. The dungeon is so much worse than you ever imagined. When a rat runs over your lap, Yan races out of your pocket to pounce on it.

"Yan?" whispers Dame Scotia.

"Yes," you reply. "You told me it's always good to have a cat for the road."

"This changes everything!" she announces. Her voice is still weak, but you hear a spark of excitement.

Dame Scotia picks up Yan and holds her near her face. She speaks to her with the purrs and meows of a cat. Yan meows back, then leaps to the ground. She slips easily between the bars of the dungeon and heads up the stairs.

Go on to the next page.

"We're going to be okay." Dame Scotia squeezes your hand. "Yan will bring us bits of food *and* kill the rats in here. When I get stronger, I'll be able to use her to get us out of here."

Sure enough, Yan delivers scraps of food she's stolen from the kitchen. Over the next several days, Dame Scotia's health gradually improves, and yours worsens only a little.

Then, one day, Lord Padraig and Dame Tira come down to the dungeon.

"You're looking better, my dear," he tells Dame Scotia. "Are you sure you won't change your mind?"

"Never!" she replies. "I will die before I make you a pegacorn army!"

"And your assistant?" he asks.

"Never!" you reply.

Lord Padraig unlocks the dungeon and yanks you out. Dame Scotia tucks Yan behind her and tells you, "Be brave!"

Turn to the next page.

Lord Padraig and Dame Tira drag you upstairs and out to the unicorn paddock. You've been in the dungeon for so long that the sunlight hurts your eyes, but you inhale the fresh air eagerly. Lord Padraig brings you to a unicorn and says, "This unicorn comes from Flanders, just like you. It's done very well here, don't you think?"

You are still blinking as your eyes adjust, but the unicorn does seem healthy.

Lord Padraig pulls a knife out of his robe and holds it to the unicorn's neck. The unicorn's eyes widen with terror.

"Don't!" you shout.

"It's up to you," says Lord Padraig. "If you sew pegacorn wings, the unicorn lives. If you refuse, I'm perfectly willing to sacrifice this unicorn."

Your heart stops. You know Dame Scotia doesn't want you to sew wings for him, but how can you let a unicorn die? Even if you sew the wings, how will they work without Dame Scotia's magic?

If you agree to sew wings to save the unicorn's life, turn to page 96.

If you still refuse to sew wings, turn to page 112.

With one final glance at Dame Scotia, you know that you can't stand by and let her suffer. "I'll sew wings starting tomorrow morning, but only if you bring Dame Scotia some food and water right now," you tell Lord Padraig. After all, if Dame Scotia won't use her magic, the wings you make are probably useless. You may as well make sure she is fed.

You hear Dame Scotia starting to cry. Does she *want* to die?

When the food is brought, she does sit up and eat, but she won't meet your eyes. You understand that she feels you are betraying her, but you believe you're doing the right thing.

For the next two days, you sew wings, exactly the same way you did in Edinburgh for Dame Scotia when she turned cats into pegacorns. Dame Tira comes over to observe from time to time and praises your stitches.

"You know, Dame Scotia turns cats, not unicorns, into pegacorns," you tell her.

"I know," says Dame Tira. "Cats are her magical domain, but I hate them. I'm going to have to see if I can turn a unicorn into a pegacorn. I think it can't be that hard, although I'm not used to working with unicorns."

That gives you an idea. The next time Yan scampers onto your lap, you whisper, "I'm sorry," and pull out a bit of her fur. She howls, jumps off you, and races out of the room.

Turn to page 80.

80

Carefully, you sew tiny pieces of cat fur into the wings. Mixed with the white feathers, they are impossible to detect, and you can't help feeling proud of your work. But will it thwart Dame Tira's magic?

When a pair of wings is complete, Lord Padraig, Dame Tira, and you take them to the unicorn paddock. The three of you walk among the thirteen unicorns as Dame Tira examines them.

"Not this one," she says of a green-eyed unicorn. "This was one of my sister's cats before she turned it into a unicorn. I don't want to have her magic mixed up with my own."

Dame Tira selects a unicorn with pale gray eyes and leads it out of the paddock. Lord Padraig forces it to sit, and you place the wings on its back. You're relieved that the cat fur can't be seen at all.

Dame Tira shakes her hair over the wings, just as Dame Scotia does for her spell, except tiny crescent moons, not stars, tumble out. Curiously, they bounce back from the wings and hover above the feathers.

You try to conceal a smile. Dame Tira stops abruptly and says, "It's not working. The magic is being forced back from the wings."

"Keep trying," Lord Padraig urges her. You can barely contain your excitement! Is it possible Yan's cat fur is destroying Dame Tira's magic?

Still nothing happens, and Dame Tira tries a third time. Now you don't care who sees you smile.

Go on to the next page.

"Maybe a different unicorn is what we need," says Dame Tira. The spell is unsuccessful with the second unicorn too, and your hopes expand.

She is unable to transform any of the unicorns into pegacorns!

For the next several days, Dame Scotia continues to be fed, while her sister tries reworking her spells. You sew a second set of wings, but again you secretly add a little cat fur, and the spell fails.

"I can't do it," Dame Tira finally admits to Lord Padraig. "I *do* have magical skills, but it's going to take time for me to explore how to create a pegacorn. In the meantime, please let my sister go. She is as stubborn as stone; she is never going to make pegacorns for you, but I can continue trying."

Lord Padraig smiles warmly at Dame Tira. Suddenly you wonder, is it possible he's fallen in love with her? "Fine, my dear. I don't need a corpse in the dungeon anyway."

You can barely contain your joy, but then Dame Tira says, "Let me keep my sister's assistant here; I may need wings when I get this spell worked out."

"As you wish," Lord Padraig replies, and your heart plummets.

"Wait!" you cry. "Let me go back to Edinburgh too!"

No one even listens to your words.

Turn to page 117.

"I think you're right, Captain Hullett. I will join your crew!" You kiss the baby unicorn goodbye, pick up Eleanor, and return to the ship. You try not to think about Dame Scotia and the possibility of a pegacorn army.

Your voyages take you to fascinating cities in more countries than you knew existed. You go back to Flanders several times and are delighted to visit your village again. You always have your eye out for unicorns, and sometimes you check the sky for pegacorns. However, you never see a unicorn again.

The End

You still feel uncertain as you get out of bed, but you decide that trusting Susannah is your best option. She leads you through the castle to a stable, where she gestures to one of the largest horses you've ever seen and asks, "Can you ride?" You hesitate. You have a lot more experience riding unicorns than horses, and this horse looks huge.

Without waiting for your answer, Susannah puts a bridle on the horse and says, "Never mind. We don't have time for riding lessons. Get on behind me." She blows out the candle, climbs on the horse, and pulls you up.

There is just a sliver of moon, so the horse has to step carefully in the darkness.

"How did you get the silver moons in your hair?" you ask Susannah.

"I stole them from Dame Tira," she replies proudly, "and I can tell you that wasn't easy!"

Her words assure you that you made the right decision! "You know they're magical," you tell Susannah.

"That's why I stole them."

Turn to the next page.

There is a hint of pink on the horizon when Susannah and you dismount. She ties the horse to a tree and says, "We're walking the rest of the way."

The guards by Lord Padraig's castle are sleeping when you arrive. You are tempted to sneak by them, but Susannah shakes one awake and says, "Good sir, we are the new servants. We are meant to help with breakfast."

The guard sleepily waves you inside. It's still very dark in the castle, but you follow the sounds of chopping to the kitchen. The kitchen is larger than your entire cottage in Flanders! You curtsy to the workers and again introduce yourselves as the new servants.

Go on to the next page.

"About time we got some help in here!" says one of the cooks. "All the lord thinks about is unicorn-this, unicorn-that. And now we have a lady in the dungeon! Do we feed her like a lady or like a prisoner?"

"You feed her as lady," you reply with assurance. "When she gets out of the dungeon, she will remember your respect."

"When she gets out—hah!" scoffs the cook. "Still, better safe than sorry. Since you know so much about feeding ladies, put together a nice breakfast for her and take it to the dungeon. Better bring the guard there something special too or the lady will never get that breakfast."

Turn to the next page.

86

You and Susannah each prepare a tray with apples, nuts, and oatcakes. There's a mug of mead on each tray too. The cook points you toward a staircase down to the dungeon.

Halfway down the winding steps, Susannah stops and puts down her tray. "Make sure you are the one to bring breakfast to Dame Scotia." She pulls a tiny pouch from her pocket and sprinkles its contents into the cup of mead, then stirs it with her finger. She wipes the finger on her tunic, picks up the tray, and continues down the steps.

"Good morning!" she greets the dungeon guard enthusiastically. "Lord Padraig ordered both you and the prisoner to have a special breakfast."

In the faint light from his lantern, you see the guard grinning.

"We'll need you to open the cell to bring the prisoner breakfast," you tell him.

The guard removes a key from a ring dangling from his belt and leads you past a row of empty cells to one where you see Dame Scotia huddled in a corner. He unlocks the door so you can enter.

You place the tray on the floor beside her. It's so dark inside that you're not sure she can recognize you, so you speak. "Good morning, good lady."

Turn to page 88.

You hear her gasp, but she controls her voice when she replies, "Thank you." She grabs your wrist, and runs the fingers of her other hand through her hair until she finds a silver star. She places it in your hand and closes your fingers around it into a fist.

You and Susannah do not return to the kitchen. You wait halfway up the stairs until you hear the guard snoring. Then you creep back to the dungeon, take the key, and let Dame Scotia out of her cell.

"I hope Dame Scotia knows how to ride a horse," whispers Susannah. "I'm staying here to deal with Lord Padraig or else she will never be free from him. Besides, I need to steal some unicorns."

You press the silver star into her hand. Your heart is full of gratitude and relief, but all you manage to say is "Thank you, Susannah!" Then you and Dame Scotia sneak out of the castle into the bright morning light.

The End

Running as fast as you can over the rocks, you hurry back to Yan.

To your surprise, she's not in the meadow!

"Yan! Yan!" you call, trying to not panic.

Could I possibly have returned to a different meadow? you wonder, but no, you feel pretty certain this is exactly where you left Yan. You pace methodically all over the meadow looking for signs of the unicorn. The flapping of an eagle overhead momentarily spooks you, and you ask yourself if an eagle could have carried Yan off, but it doesn't seem likely. She wasn't *that* small! You know there are wolves in Scotland, but you don't see any traces of blood.

You call her name again and again until your throat hurts. You start searching in the woods. Hours pass, and there is no sign of the little unicorn.

Feeling utterly defeated, you force yourself to walk toward Edinburgh. Yan is gone, and you can't help feeling responsible. Not only that, you traded Eleanor to Hendon, and if she ever finds out, Dame Scotia won't be pleased. You think back to how many times Dame Scotia urged you not to get involved. Then, in a flash, you know your time in Scotland is over.

Back in the city, you gather the remaining white cats to say goodbye, then count out three silver coins from Dame Scotia's stash, and head to the harbor. You take the next boat back to Flanders.

The End

You have to duck your head to enter the cave, and suddenly one foot plunges into nothingness! You find yourself falling, falling, falling! You land in a heap on rocks, and pain shoots up both your legs.

Where *are* you? Glowing lights are shifting around you, and you hear the sounds of feathers rustling. As your eyes adjust, you realize you are surrounded by winged beings! Could they be angels?

Am I dead? you ask yourself.

As they come closer, you see the agony in their faces, and understand you are seeing the *sluagh*, the unforgiven dead. Their feathery wings brush against your face. Your last breath is filled with fear.

The End

"Excuse me, Lord Padraig, but I can sew a wing very well," you announce.

Dame Scotia looks at you with exasperation, but Lord Padraig eyes you with curiosity.

"Is that so?" he chuckles. To his servants he says, "Take the two of them to a guest chamber. Maybe the red one would be most suitable. Bring them plenty of food."

A servant leads the two of you inside the castle. You are supposed to follow her, but you hesitate to step on a rug so beautifully woven that soiling it with your shoes seems very wrong. You pause to admire the ivy and rose pattern of the rug, then notice the tapestries adorning the walls. For a second, you imagine yourself living in such grandeur, but then Dame Scotia pulls your hand.

"Let me be clear," she whispers to you, "we are *not* creating a flying army! Don't think you are doing me any favors by sewing some wings."

"I don't want you to end up in a dungeon!"

Dame Scotia stops walking and stares at you. "Do you think I am not magical enough to handle a dungeon? I will be fine. However, I may not have enough magic to help *you* in a dungeon."

For the first time, you realize that your presence has actually complicated Dame Scotia's situation. You only wanted to rescue her, but have you accidentally made her escape more difficult?

Turn to the next page.

That night, you eat rich foods you have never tasted before. There are sweet fruits, all unfamiliar, and savory sauces. You chew meat from animals you can't identify and sample salty cheese. With the fullest belly you have ever had, you go to sleep in a bed draped with red velvet.

The next day a servant leads you to a workshop. There are bolts of cloth and baskets of feathers. You find the right size needle, unwind some thread, and get to work. By dinnertime, you finish one wing.

Go on to the next page.

Again there is a sumptuous meal, but Dame Scotia refuses to even look at you, and you understand that she feels you have betrayed her. As you pull the velvet covers up to your chin that night, you wonder if you're doing the right thing.

"Dame Scotia," you whisper in the darkness, "just because we make pegacorns doesn't mean he will have a flying army. Pegacorns can fly away."

There is silence, and then she says, "You have a point. Let me think about this."

The next day you finish sewing the second wing, and Dame Scotia cheerfully announces she will turn one of the unicorns into a pegacorn. Lord Padraig says it can wait until morning, but she insists it's best to do it while the wings are fresh.

You're confused. You almost always fly the pegacorns in the morning, and certainly never at night.

As you, Dame Scotia, and Lord Padraig walk toward the unicorn paddock, she tells you, "Go choose a unicorn for me, ideally one with green eyes."

You stroll among the unicorns, patting their backs and checking their eyes, until you come to one with blue eyes. You gaze at it intently, and the unicorn meets your eyes. Could this really be the one taken from Flanders? You kiss its nose and whisper, "I have not forgotten you." Then you resume looking until you find a green-eyed unicorn to lead out of the paddock to Dame Scotia.

Turn to the next page.

You know the steps involved with creating a pegacorn, but this is the first time Dame Scotia is creating one from a unicorn, not a cat. You wonder if she will even succeed. Nonetheless, you guide the green-eyed unicorn to lie down, and place the wings on either side of its back. Dame Scotia runs her fingers through her matted curls and shakes out a few silver stars, letting them fall onto the unicorn. You listen to her murmur the words you've heard many times, but never been able to completely catch.

You watch as the feathered wings attach themselves to the unicorn's back. The surprised pegacorn scrambles to her feet and tentatively flaps her wings. Even though you've seen this before, you gasp with delight. A new pegacorn never fails to thrill you!

Lord Padraig is beaming. "My Lord, please do me the honor of being the first to ride this pegacorn," says Dame Scotia as she sweeps her arm dramatically toward the new creature. You are a little surprised, because it's always been *your* job to introduce new pegacorns to the sky. You look around for a bridle, but, sensing your intention, Dame Scotia shakes her head.

Lord Padraig clumsily climbs onto the pegacorn and kicks his heels against her sides. "Let's go!" he snaps as he clutches the mane.

Go on to the next page.

The pegacorn takes a few steps, flapping its wings, and then with one big swoosh is airborne. Lord Padraig laughs loudly.

When the pegacorn is nearly as high as the castle tower, Dame Scotia waves her hand and calls, "Lord Padraig, say hello from the sky!"

Still laughing, Lord Padraig waves one hand with excitement. Dame Scotia now waves both her hands in the air. Lord Padraig does too, but at that instant the pegacorn lurches, and he tumbles off. You watch him grab the pegacorn's leg, but she kicks his hand loose. Lord Padraig lands with a deadly thump and the pegacorn soars away from the castle.

You realize you are free! You grab Dame Scotia's hand and say, "Get on one of the unicorns. We're riding out of here right now!" You climb onto the blue-eyed unicorn and press your heels into its sides.

While Lord Padraig's servants gather around his broken body, you and Dame Scotia race away from the castle, all the way back to Edinburgh.

The End

"Stop!" you shout. "I'll sew wings, but do not kill the unicorn!"

Dame Tira puts her arm around you. "That's a wise decision. Now, get to work."

You sew feathers onto wings, just as you used to do in Edinburgh for Dame Scotia. You keep hoping Yan will come visit you, but she doesn't. You tell yourself it's just as well Dame Scotia has the kitten for comfort.

Finally, when a pair is finished, Lord Padraig, Dame Tira, and you head out to the unicorn paddock. Dame Tira wanders around the unicorns to find one she wants to use. Lord Padraig leads it out of the fenced paddock and makes it lie down. You drape the wings over its back and step back to watch. You consider pointing out that Dame Scotia always transformed cats, not unicorns, into pegacorns, but you don't want to do anything to help Dame Tira's magic succeed, so you say nothing.

Dame Tira shakes her fox-colored curls over the unicorn and tiny crescent moons fall onto the wings. It's just like what Dame Scotia did when she turned cats into pegacorns, only her hair was full of stars. Dame Tira chants words you can't understand. Slowly, the feathers and the unicorn fur weave themselves together. The unicorn tentatively flaps its new wings and stumbles to its feet.

"Well done, my dear!" says Lord Padraig, and he kisses Dame Tira's hand.

Turn to page 98.

You fight back tears. You can't believe you've helped create a pegacorn army. Dame Scotia would be heartbroken, but you never see her again, so you're not sure she knows.

Sure enough, within a year, Lord Padraig's flying army enables him to easily take over all of Scotland.

You are resigned to your work. One morning, you are about to pluck a feather from the basket to start sewing another wing, when you notice a silver star on top. You examine it closely. It's exactly like those in Dame Scotia's hair! How could it have gotten here?

You never know for sure, but you tell yourself that Dame Scotia left it there to tell you that she and Yan were escaping. That's what you want to believe.

The End

You lower your eyes as two men lead Dame Scotia away.

Lord Padraig gestures toward you and says, "Take this one to the unicorn keeper. If this orphan is useful, fine. If not, send the child away."

A servant not much older than you takes your hand and leads you around the outside of the castle to the back. You can't believe your eyes! There's a fenced paddock filled with unicorns. You pause to count them—thirteen! They all look vibrant and healthy, prancing around and swishing their tails.

The servant takes you to a tall and slender man with gentle eyes and light brown hair, and tells him, "Tommy, our lord thinks this Flemish orphan may be useful with the unicorns, but if not, good riddance."

"Welcome," says the unicorn keeper. "Go find the dirtiest unicorn and give it a good cleaning." He hands you a brush.

You wander into the paddock, and for a moment you are so happy to be surrounded by unicorns that you completely forget about Dame Scotia in the dungeon. All the unicorns appear very well groomed, so you spend your time carefully examining each one.

Turn to the next page.

102

There's a unicorn that's freckled with silver spots, something you've never seen before. You notice one has green eyes, and understand that this unicorn started life as one of Dame Scotia's cats. Another unicorn has deep black eyes and strands of black running through its mane. Then you see one with eyes that match the sky. This jolts you back to the memory of the Flemish unicorn being loaded on a boat in Bruges. Could it possibly be the same unicorn?

You start with what seems to be the oldest unicorn, brushing its coat until it gleams. You braid the mane and tail, tucking wildflowers into the plait.

"You love unicorns," Tommy says as he inspects your work. "I'll find you a place to sleep in the stable. Come, I'll make sure you have a good dinner after your journey here." You feel grateful for his kindness.

That night, you sleep on a bed of straw in the stable, surrounded by thirteen gently snoring unicorns. It's not the most comfortable bed you've ever had, but you are quite content. You try to imagine how Dame Scotia must be suffering.

Go on to the next page.

The next morning, Lord Padraig and Dame Scotia arrive at the paddock. Her hair is a tangled mess, and you don't see any stars sparkling among her curls. Her scarlet dress is smudged with dirt, and she looks like she hasn't slept. You try to catch her eye, but she glances away.

Tommy, the unicorn keeper, bows and says, "The orphan is a natural with unicorns, and a very hard worker. I welcome this assistance, my Lord!"

"I'm glad to hear that," says Lord Padraig. He takes Dame Scotia by the arm and says, "I want to see you try. These unicorns are going to fly no matter what." You tense up when he grabs her arm, but remain where you are standing.

She sighs and enters the paddock. She strolls among the unicorns until she finds the green-eyed one. "Oh, Nomi!" she whispers, stroking its mane. "How many years has it been since I last saw you?"

"That one," orders Lord Padraig. "Turn that unicorn into one that flies."

Turn to the next page.

Dame Scotia smiles slyly. She runs her fingers through her curls until she pulls out a small silver star, which she places on the unicorn's forehead just below the horn. She starts to sing in a language you can't understand, touching the unicorn on its head, its back, its flanks, and combing her fingers through its mane. The unicorn starts to shrink, and as its horn disappears, its coat grows into long fur. By the time the song ends, the green-eyed unicorn is a green-eyed cat.

You see the look on Lord Padraig's face and hurry forward. "This is what she can do," you tell him. "Cats to unicorns and unicorns back to cats. She isn't skilled with wings."

Lord Padraig stutters with fury. "I-I-I don't need a cat!" he shouts as he kicks Nomi. The white cat dashes out of the paddock.

"Run home, Nomi! Run home!" Dame Scotia calls.

Lord Padraig leads Dame Scotia away. You wonder what you can you do to help, but you have unicorns to tend to. You make sure every mane and every tail is silky smooth. You brush the dust off every horn. When you think each unicorn looks absolutely perfect, Tommy suggests you inspect their hooves.

Go on to the next page.

That afternoon, when Dame Scotia and Lord Padraig return, a servant runs up holding two swan wings, still dripping blood.

Dame Scotia turns away with horror. "The blood!" she shrieks. "That will never work." She looks Lord Padraig in the eye. "You have all these unicorns, but don't even know that unicorn blood isn't red!"

The lord is momentarily surprised. You see Tommy roll his eyes.

"Take me back to the dungeon," she snaps. "I'm not touching those wings."

It is the last time you ever see Dame Scotia.

You and Tommy become good friends, and the unicorns love you. If you weren't worried about Dame Scotia, you would be completely happy. After a few weeks, you summon the courage to ask Tommy what happened to her.

Tommy puts his arm around your shoulders and shakes his head. "These unicorns were never meant to be weapons. She is a brave woman." Then he corrects himself. "She *was* a brave woman." He hugs you as you cry.

The End

"Thank you, Your Highness," you tell the Queen, nodding your head. "I would be honored to serve you!"

A smile fills the Queen's face. "We are going to be wonderful friends!"

After a short battle, the King conquers Lord Padraig and rescues Dame Scotia. When you are in Edinburgh, you and Eleanor visit her, but in fact, as Queen Margaret's closest friend, you travel all over Scotland. Queen Margaret faces many tragedies, and you are always at her side. When the King is killed two years later and the Queen becomes the ruler of Scotland, she relies on your common sense to help her govern.

Liss is the last pegacorn ever created. You visit him every day and remember your life with Dame Scotia. Every now and then, you think back to your simple life in a small village in Flanders, and marvel that now, you sit beside a queen!

The End

"Thank you, Captain Hullett," you say, "but I'll wait for the Archbishop to return."

"As you wish! Good luck!" He waves goodbye, and you hug the baby unicorn more tightly. Eleanor flicks her tail.

Over the next week, you take care of the baby unicorn as tenderly as if it had been the Queen's child. The servants are so impressed with your devotion to the unicorn that they don't give you many other chores to do. The hours fly by as you play with the unicorn, but Dame Scotia is always in the back of your mind, and you wonder when the Archbishop will return. You know that every day that passes makes the possibility of rescuing Dame Scotia less likely.

After two weeks pass, you ask the servants if they know anything more about when the Archbishop will return.

"We thought he would be back by now," one tells you. "Maybe he's gone on to Glasgow."

"Or Flanders!" suggests another. "Don't forget how much he liked that part of the world!"

Turn to page 109.

"He could return tomorrow. We really don't know," says a third.

You start to lose track of the days, and it's only when Eleanor gives birth to five snowy kittens that you realize months have passed. The baby unicorn follows you everywhere and comes when you call. This creature is the joy of your life, and Eleanor's kittens only make everything even more fun. You never forget Dame Scotia, but you realize that even when the Archbishop returns, it will probably be too late to rescue her. You try to focus on the happiness in your new life and not think about what's happening to her.

The End

"Give me a minute," you tell Susannah. "I'll meet you by the unicorn tapestries."

"Be quick," she whispers and hurries off.

You nuzzle Yan and put her in your pocket. As quietly as you can, you sneak through the dark castle to the stable. There are so many horses, but you finally find the stall containing the pegacorn.

You are leading Liss out of the stable when a guard catches you!

"*THIEF!*" he shouts. "THIEF! Someone is stealing the pegacorn!"

Bells are clanging! Lanterns glow. Before you can say a word, someone grabs you from behind.

Later, you try to explain, but Lord Eòsaph is unforgiving. Dame Tira gloats. You are locked in a room for a few days until Susannah rescues Dame Scotia herself. With many apologies and a lot of begging, Dame Scotia gets you released. The two of you go back to Edinburgh, leaving Liss as a gift to Lord Eòsaph.

The End

"Thank you, Your Highness," you tell the Queen, "but I'd really like to join the battle against Lord Padraig. I want to help rescue Dame Scotia. Maybe when we return home victoriously, I can join you."

"You are very brave!" exclaims the Queen. "I think it is a dangerous decision, and I will keep your cat safe with me."

The next morning, you are still sleepy from the banquet. Dressed as a royal soldier, you ride one of the smaller horses to Lord Padraig's castle. The King flies on Liss above, leading the army.

By the time you reach a castle with unicorn flags flying from its towers, armed men are already racing toward the royal army. Arrows whiz past you. Wounded men scream and horses groan.

You are shaking with terror! You've never even seen a battle, never mind been in the middle of one! You force yourself to continue riding toward the castle.

The arrow that pierces your chest knocks you off the horse. The last things you sense are the thunder of hooves and the blue of the sky above.

The End

112

"I won't sew wings," you tell Lord Padraig, "but please don't kill the unicorn!" You grab his arm, but he easily shakes you off.

Even though you squeeze your eyes shut, of course you hear the scream of the terrified unicorn. It's the worst moment of your life.

By the time you are back in the dungeon with Dame Scotia, you can hardly speak. She tries to console you, but hours pass before you can bring yourself to tell her what happened.

Go on to the next page.

"He is a beast!" she exclaims. "I knew he was cruel, but this is really unforgivable."

"What can we do?" you ask, still sobbing.

"I hope I'm strong enough for this," she replies. She scoops Yan into her lap. "Look through my hair. Take out as many stars as you can find, at least a dozen."

You run your fingers through Dame Scotia's curls, plucking out silver stars.

"I have twenty," you tell her, "and there are still more."

"Good! Save some for our escape."

Dame Scotia arranges the stars over Yan's little body, then says, "Come, put your hands on her back. You are still growing, and that energy could be useful."

You are excited to be part of the magic! You place your hands over Yan's star-covered fur, and Dame Scotia puts hers on top of yours. When she starts to chant, her voice is stronger than you expected.

Under your fingers, you feel Yan's silky fur start to roughen. Muscles develop, and your fingers have to spread to cover her body. Curiously, the stars are dissolving as Yan grows bigger and bigger. Dame Scotia's voice weakens, but Yan continues to grow until she is much larger than a regular cat.

"How big is she going to get?" you ask with amazement.

Turn to the next page.

114

Dame Scotia just continues to chant. When Yan is the size of a fully grown lynx, she stops and begins to speak to the enormous cat in a language you can't understand. Then Dame Scotia tells you the plan.

When you hear footsteps descending the stairs, Yan curls up in the corner. You and Dame Scotia try to hide her with your own bodies. Good thing it's dark!

As a servant unlocks the dungeon to bring you a bit of food, you and Dame Scotia move aside so Yan can leap forward. The giant cat knocks the servant down and bounds up the stairs.

You yank the stunned servant into the dungeon. You and Dame Scotia rush out, locking the door behind you. As quickly as you can, you make your way out of the castle.

Go on to the next page.

Once you are safely out of view, you ask her, "What about Yan?"

Dame Scotia sighs. "We probably won't see Yan again. She may not survive her attack on Padraig, but if she does, she will have no trouble returning to Edinburgh. Tell me, didn't you come here on Liss?"

"Right!" you exclaim.

Liss is still tied to the tree by the shore. He lifts his head from grazing and neighs with what you think is happiness.

You and Dame Scotia travel back to Edinburgh, sometimes flying, sometimes riding, and sometimes walking to give Liss a break. Weeks later, you hear that Lord Padraig was killed by a giant white cat, but you never see Yan again.

The End

"I'm honored," you tell the Queen, "but I have a chance to explore the world! Now that I know the King will rescue Dame Scotia, I think this is the time for me to leave Scotland."

The Queen pouts. "Your departure will be a loss to our nation." Then she pets Eleanor and asks, "May I have your cat to remind me of you?"

This is the second time today someone has asked for Eleanor! You hesitate. Eleanor appears to enjoy being a royal cat, but she is not really yours to give away.

"Eleanor belongs to Dame Scotia, not me. I'll leave her with you, but Dame Scotia may want her back."

When Captain Hullett's ship leaves Edinburgh the next morning, you are in the galley, making breakfast for the crew. You travel north to St. Andrews, then cross the North Sea.

Turn to page 119.

In fact, no one pays very much attention to you at all, so it's not hard to sneak out of the castle when Dame Scotia is released. You show her where Liss is waiting, and the two of you fly back to Edinburgh.

"You're not safe here," she says as the two of you take Liss into the stable. "Lord Padraig and my sister will guess that you're here with me. I hate to see you leave, but I think you should go home to Flanders."

You know that Dame Scotia is right, but you really don't want to leave!

As if he understands her words, Liss nuzzles you sadly. You stroke his horn fondly and fight back tears. You can't imagine a life without unicorns, pegacorns, magical cats, and Dame Scotia.

"Why don't you take Liss with you?" Dame Scotia suggests. "Let him rest tonight, and tomorrow you can fly home."

Liss whinnies with pleasure, and now you're sure he understands! You tell yourself that introducing a pegacorn to your homeland could be very exciting, and as it turns out, you're right. You and Liss become a sensation in Flanders, more famous than even the King! Everyone clamors to see you two and wants to know your story. You are too busy to miss Scotland!

The End

Over your years at sea, you lose count of the cities you visit. You encounter many amazing things—icebergs, whales, the night sky flaming pink and green with northern lights—but the only place you ever see unicorns again is in Edinburgh. Every time the ship docks there, you visit Dame Scotia (who the King rescued, of course!) and the cats, and if there's enough time, you sew a set of wings so Dame Scotia can create another pegacorn.

The End

ABOUT THE ARTISTS

Illustrator: Suzanne Nugent received her BFA in illustration from Moore College of Art & Design in Philadelphia, Pennsylvania. She now resides with her husband, Fred, in Philadelphia and works as a freelance illustrator. She first discovered her love for *Choose Your Own Adventure*® books when she was only four years old, which inspired her to become an artist.

Cover Artist: Marco Cannella was born in Ascoli Piceno, Italy, on September 29, 1972. Marco started his career in art as a decorator and an illustrator when he was a college student. He became a full-time professional in 2001 when he received the flag-prize for the "Palio della Quintana" (one of the most important Italian historical games). Since then, he has worked as an illustrator at Studio Inventario in Bologna. He has also been a scenery designer for professional theater companies. He works for the production company ASP srl in Rome as a character designer and set designer on the preproduction of a CG feature film. In 2004 he moved to Bangalore, India, to serve as full-time art director on this project. In 2005 he moved to Hawaii where he continues to work as a children's book illustrator and painter.

ABOUT THE AUTHOR

Deborah Lerme Goodman grew up in New York, where she saw *The Hunt of the Unicorn* tapestries that inspired a lifetime's fascination. Those amazing textiles also inspired her to study tapestry weaving in college! Aside from her two other *Unicorn* titles, she has written three other books in the original *Choose Your Own Adventure* series. She lives with her husband in Cambridge, Massachusetts, where she teaches English to adult immigrants.

For games, activities, and other fun stuff,
or to write to Deborah Lerme Goodman,
visit us online at CYOA.com

The History of Gamebooks

Although the *Choose Your Own Adventure®* series, first published in 1976, may be the best-known example of gamebooks, it was not the first.

In 1941, the legendary Argentine writer Jorge

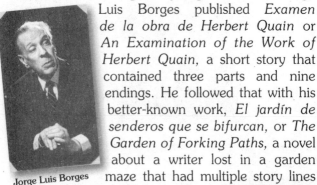

Luis Borges published *Examen de la obra de Herbert Quain* or *An Examination of the Work of Herbert Quain,* a short story that contained three parts and nine endings. He followed that with his better-known work, *El jardín de senderos que se bifurcan,* or *The Garden of Forking Paths,* a novel about a writer lost in a garden maze that had multiple story lines and endings.

Jorge Luis Borges

More than 20 years later, in 1964, another famous Argentine writer, Julio Cortázar, published a novel called *Rayuela* or *Hopscotch.* This book was composed of 155 "chapters" and the reader could make their way through a number

Julio Cortázar

of different "novels" depending on choices they made. At the same time, French author Raymond Queneau wrote an interactive story entitled *Un conte à votre façon,* or *A Story As You Like It.*

Early in the 1970s, a popular series for children called *Trackers* was published in the UK that contained multiple choices and endings. In 1976,

Journey Under the Sea,
1st Edition

R. A. Montgomery wrote and published the first gamebook for young adults: *Journey Under the Sea* under the series name *The Adventures of You*. This was changed to *Choose Your Own Adventure* by Bantam Books when they published this and five others to launch the series in 1979. The success of CYOA spawned many imitators and the term gamebooks came into use to refer to any books that utilized the second person "you" to tell a story using multiple choices and endings.

Montgomery said in an interview in 2013: "This wasn't traditional literature. The *New York Times* children's book reviewer called *Choose Your Own Adventure* a literary movement. Indeed it was. The most important thing for me has always been to get kids reading. It's not the format, it's not even the writing. The reading happened because kids were in the driver's seat. They were the mountain climber, they were the doctor, they were the deep-sea explorer. They made choices, and so they read. There were people who expressed the feeling that nonlinear literature wasn't 'normal.' But interactive books have a long history, going back 70 years."

Young R. A. Montgomery

Choose Your Own Adventure Timeline

1977 – R. A. Montgomery writes *Journey Under the Sea* under the pen name Robert Mountain. It is published by Vermont Crossroads Press along with the title *Sugar Cane Island* under the series name *The Adventures of You*.

1979 – Montgomery brings his book series to New York where it is rejected by 14 publishers before being purchased by Bantam Books for the brand new children's division. The new series is renamed *Choose Your Own Adventure*.

1980 – *Space and Beyond* initial sales are slow until Bantam seeds libraries across the U.S. with 100,000 free copies.

1983 – CYOA sales reach ten million units of the first 14 titles.

1984 – For a six-week period, 9 spots of the top 15 books on the Waldenbooks Children's Bestsellers list belong to CYOA. *Choose* dominates the list throughout the 1980s.

1989 – Ten years after its original publication, over 150 CYOA titles have been published.

1990 – R. A. Montgomery publishes the *TRIO* series with Bantam, a six-book series that draws inspiration

from future worlds in CYOA titles *Escape* and *Beyond Escape*.

1992 – ABC TV adapts Shannon Gilligan's CYOA title *The Case of the Silk King* as a made-for-TV movie. It is set in Thailand and stars Pat Morita, Soleil Moon Frye and Chad Allen.

1995 – A horror trend emerges in the children's book market, and Bantam launches *Choose Your Own Nightmare*, a series of shorter CYOA titles focused on creepy themes. The subseries is translated into several languages and converted to DVD and computer games.

1998 – Bantam licenses property from *Star Wars* to release *Choose Your Own Star Wars Adventures*. The 3-book series features traditional CYOA elements to place the reader in each of the existing *Star Wars* films and features holograms on the covers.

2003 – With the series virtually out of print, the copyright licenses and the *Choose Your Own Adventure* trademark revert to R. A. Montgomery. He forms Chooseco LLC with Shannon Gilligan.

2005 – *Choose Your Own Adventure* is re-launched into the education market, with all new art and covers. Texts have been updated to reflect changes to technology and discoveries in archaeology and science.

2006 – Chooseco LLC, operating out of a renovated farmhouse in Waitsfield, Vermont, publishes the series for the North American retail market, shipping 900,000 copies in its first six months.

2008 – Chooseco publishes CYOA *The Golden Path*, a three volume epic for readers 10+, written by Anson Montgomery.

2008 – Poptropica and Chooseco partner to develop the first branded Poptropica island, "Nabooti Island," based on CYOA #4, *The Lost Jewels of Nabooti*.

2009 – *Choose Your Own Adventure* celebrates 30 years in print and releases two titles in partnership with WADA, the World Anti-Doping Agency, to emphasize fairness in sport.

2010 – Chooseco launches a new look for the classic books using special neon ink.

2013 – Chooseco launches eBooks on Kindle and in the iBookstore with trackable maps and other bonus features. The project is briefly hung up when Apple has to rewrite its terms and conditions for publishers to create space for this innovative eBook type.

2014 – Brazil and Korea license publishing rights to the series. 20 foreign publishers currently distribute the series worldwide.

2014 – Beloved series founder R. A. Montgomery dies at age 78. He finishes his final book in the *Choose Your Own Adventure* series only weeks before.

2018 – Z-Man Games releases the first-ever *Choose Your Own Adventure* board game, adapted from *House of Danger*. Record sales lead to the creation of a new game for 2019 based on *War with the Evil Power Master*.

2019 – Chooseco publishes a new sub-series of *Choose Your Own Adventure* books based on real-life spies. The first two of the series are *Spies: Mata Hari* and *Spies: James Armistead Lafayette,* by debut authors Katherine Factor and Kyandreia Jones.

2020 – Chooseco publishes baby books adapted from the first 3 CYOA classics and they are so popular a full reprint is ordered two months ahead of publication.

2021 – Fall sees two ground-breaking longer, bigger books in the series, the side-splittingly funny *Time Travel Inn* by Bart King, and the evocative young adult fantasy novel *The Citadel of Whispers* by Kazim Ali.

CHOOSE YOUR OWN ADVENTURE®
BOX SETS

4 or 6 books
in each box!

Available at cyoa.com or ask your favorite bookstore!

THE MAGIC OF THE UNICORN

CHOOSE FROM 27 ENDINGS!

BY DEBORAH LERME GOODMAN

If you decide to go to the leper camp, turn to page 8.

If you head for the graveyard, turn to page 12.

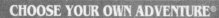

CHOOSE YOUR OWN ADVENTURE®

THE RESCUE OF THE UNICORN

CHOOSE FROM 24 ENDINGS!

BY DEBORAH LERME GOODMAN

If you decide to stay with the unicorn as it is brought to the castle, turn to page 18.

If you decide to rescue the unicorn now and try to take it back to Flanders, turn to page 38.

THE TRUMPET OF TERROR

CHOOSE
FROM 28
ENDINGS!

BY DEBORAH LERME GOODMAN

If you decide to search for Idunn before doing anything else, go on to the next page.

If you think it's best to get rid of Gullveig first, turn to page 19.

CHOOSE YOUR OWN ADVENTURE®

TIME TRAVEL Inn

"Mind-blowing adventure & heart-stopping thrills!"
- **Jeff Kinney**, *Diary of a Wimpy Kid*

Your wacky grandmother Dolores disappears into thin air and you and your family suddenly become the caretakers of her motel - Time Travel Inn. When you begin to investigate, it does not take long to figure out that the inn is an epicenter for time travel research gone very, very wrong.

Written by well-known humor author Bart King (*Bad Dad Jokes: That's How Eye Roll* and *The Pocket Guide to Mischief*).

START YOUR TRAVEL AT CYOA.COM

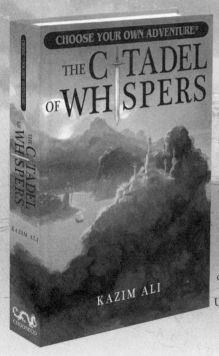

INTRODUCTION

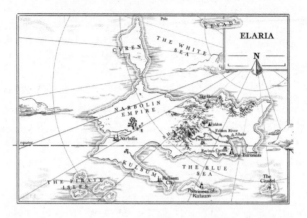

You were only ten years old when the Whisperers came to your village. Most people don't even know the Whisperers exist. Whisperers come and go in secret. They scout the entire realm for candidates, and their processes are mysterious and selective. When a candidate is identified, the parents of the child are negotiated with directly.

In your case, it was Chandh Sahib who came to the village himself, disguised as a peddler of pots and pans. He was in the kitchen of your family's modest house, speaking with your parents. Suddenly he threw off the coarse over-jacket he wore and stood up, revealing a robe of black velvet with sigils of a silver moon in all its phases stitched down the sides.

"What is this?" your father exclaimed, though your mother seemed unsurprised.

"The secret is this," Chandh Sahib said. "I represent the Whisperers, an order devoted to keeping peace in the land. We work in secret and would like to take Krishi to our school for training. We will send you money to support your family and the village, and Krishi will come back to see you once a year. None of this must be known by anyone."

You were intrigued and excited but worried your father would object. Then your mother put her hand on his. He looked over at her.

"Do you remember when I told you I had traveled across the continent in my youth?" she asked him.

He nodded.

She reached to her neck and pulled a medallion up from under her tunic. It glinted bright silver—a small crescent moon. Chandh Sahib wears an amulet just like it, but while his depicts a full moon, your mother's depicts the new crescent.

"Sister," said Chandh Sahib, nodding toward her. "I did not recognize you."

"We appear as we wish to be seen," she said, as if repeating a line she had long studied.

And so it was. You were given your *own* amulet depicting the first crescent of the moon, and you left your family and crossed the water to the Isle of the Citadel, where the ancient and infamous Citadel of Whispers is perched.

You still returned home every summer, as Chandh Sahib promised, but as the years passed, whenever you were home in your village, you found yourself longing for the twisting mountain trails and deep forested interior of the mysterious Isle of the Citadel.

In those first, heady days, you and your best friends Zara and Saeed spent countless hours exploring the labyrinthine

THE FLIGHT OF
THE UNICORN

This book is different from other books.

You and YOU ALONE are in charge of what happens in this story.

There are dangers, choices, adventures and consequences. YOU must use all of your numerous talents and much of your enormous intelligence. The wrong decision could end in disaster—even death. But don't despair. At any time, YOU can go back and make another choice, alter the path of your story, and change its result.

After a unicorn rescue mission brought you from your home in Flanders to Scotland, you're finally settling into your new life. You spend your days working as an apprentice to the brilliant Dame Scotia, who uses her magic to turn cats into pegacorns (flying unicorns)! Except, one day you arrive home and discover that Dame Scotia is missing. Is she in danger? Only YOU can track her down and save her pegacorns from a terrible fate!

VISIT US ONLINE AT CYOA.COM

INTRODUCTION

passages of the Citadel itself, but your favorite times were when you wandered alone, climbing high into the ramparts which overlooked the ocean, or else following the maze of paths deep into the woods where other and more ancient buildings of the Whisperers were rumored to be.

LIST OF CHARACTERS

AT THE CITADEL

students
…] are Krishi, a junior student
…d, a junior student
…, a junior student
…o, a junior student
…ple, a younger student
…asters
…ndh Sahib, the principal master
…dhya, the weapons master
…j, the dance master
…sitors
…n, a prospective student
…v Acharya, a Whisperer

AT THE FARMHOUSE

Shivani, the principal master
The Colonel, Shivani's secretary
Rabab, the language and diplomacy master

AT THE CACTUS FARM

Rubio and Meghan, prickly-pear cactus farmers
Tommy, their elder son
Max, their younger son
Doron, Casey, Finnegan, Alec, and Caleb, workers at the farm

AT THE MANOR HOUSE

Lowelia, the Baroness of the Two Rivers district
Javid, her castellan
Margalit, boss of the garden crew
Etheldreda, a gardener
The Duc de Berry, a member of the Guild Council
The Countess of South Cliff, a member of the Guild Council
The Marquis de Bois, a member of the Guild Council
The Dazzling Zubaydah, an entertainer
Dannel, one of the Baroness's guards

IN ALBAHR

Bobby, Robert, and Roberto, the proprietors of The Three Roberts

SOME PIRATES

Zephyr, a scoundrel
Dalilah, the Duchess of Kulsum and Captain of the Blade
Nakul and Sahadev, two sailors

3